Mysteries of Frost

Collection 5

~ *Aurora's Dapper Denouement* ~

Written by

Jana A. Bee

Illustrations by

Jo N. Bee

Copyright © 2022 Jana A. Bee All rights reserved.
KDP ISBN: 9798371372697

Copyright

Copyright © 2022 Jana A. Bee All rights reserved
KDP ISBN: 9798371372697

All characters and events are completely fictitious and do
not reflect real events or people (living, or dead) in any
form. Any resemblance is completely coincidental and not
intended by the author.

No part of this book may be reproduced, or stored in a
retrieval system, or transmitted in any form or by any
means, electronic, mechanical, photocopying, recording, or
otherwise, without express written permission of the
publisher, except for the use of brief quotations in a book
review.

To request permissions, please contact
jana.a.bee.mof@gmail.com

Cover design and Illustrations: Jo N. Bee

Dedication

Thanks~

To aspiring sleuths, science and my family!

~Jana

Aurora's Dapper Denouement

Map of Verwood

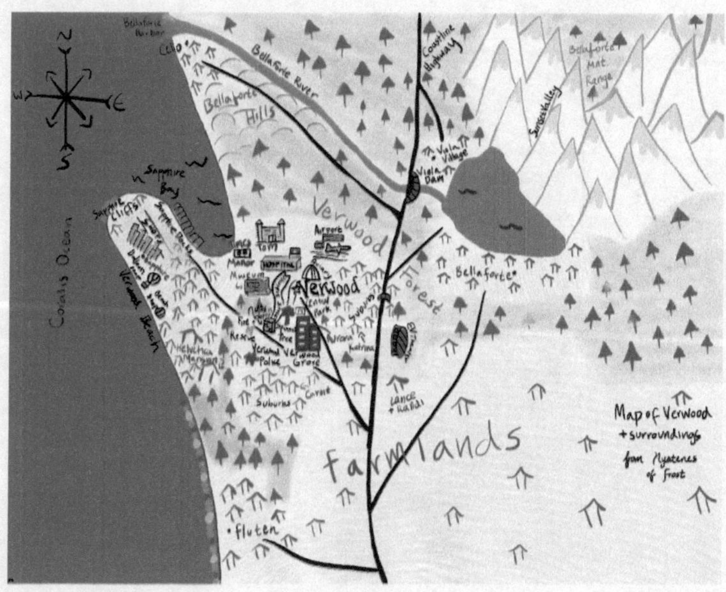

Aurora's Apartment

No. 316 Verwood Grove Apartments

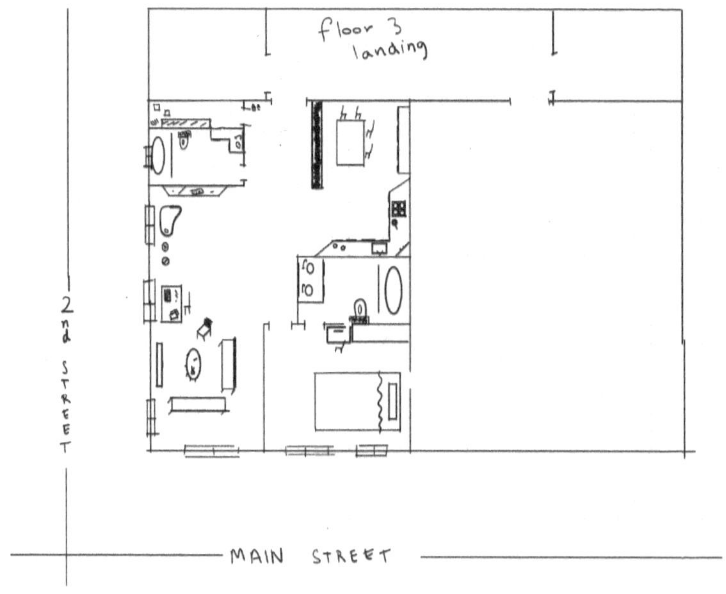

Contents

The Baker's Dozen

Felines all around

Sitting on the ground

Sleuth at midnight

No time for catfights

Aurora knows who

Prologue

Cupcakes were evidently not as easy as the instructions' title said they would be. Cupcakes involved a lot more pan-washing than the instructions mentioned.

Aurora had flour, sugar, and cocoa powder lined against the windowsill as she tried to scrub off the dried chocolate from her 10*14 pan. Scrubbing dried chocolate off pans was not exactly how Aurora had planned to spend the night a week before her birthday, but, if that's what allowed for tasty homemade cupcakes, so be it!

The piece of chocolate she was scrubbing seemed to give away at last, and she set the pan in her sink. And the sponge. And… *where did that mixing spoon go*? Aurora spotted it on the floor and proceeded to clean up that mess. She heard a bit of clanging behind her and when she turned around, spotted that the bag of flour had tipped over. Small paw prints - Snowy's paw prints - led out the window.

Aurora sighed. It was Thursday, and Snowy's disappearances always happened on Thursdays near midnight. The clock claimed the time was 11:42PM. Aurora signed again for good measure. There was no use in chasing after her comrade, since the cat was fast and the night was dark.

Leaving a window open for Snowy to crawl back through, Aurora finished cleaning up her baking mess and went to bed, looking forward to her birthday coming up soon. She was more than exasperated as she wondered where Snowy went.

The Scent

~~Snowy~~

Snowy meowed as she made the jump from the first floor to the ground. Scents allured her as she walked down an alley, then another. The scent was familiar, and tasty, yet Snowy couldn't quite place it.

She had grown used to this scent, as it had been luring her out of her home and into streets in the dark nights. This had been going on for the past few months, and slowly, Snowy resolved to figure out what this scent was. Perhaps a little bit of investigation, like *her* comrade, Aurora…

Snowy turned another corner and headed towards the Verwood's oblong park. The roadway was better lit as she crossed the street and entered. In the open lawn sat…

Something…

Snowy couldn't quite note what it was as she sat down, and took in another deep breath of the mystery scent. There were park lamps above Snowy which illuminated other cats. They seemed to be sitting in a wide circle. Snowy was also a part of the circle.

The lamps grew dimmer and dimmer as Snowy slowly… slowly… dozed off….

Chapter 1

Aurora loved to hop between the pavement's cracks. She was downtown, and the Friday afternoon was slightly chilly. The plan was to go by *Apples Cores* and get a warm cup of tea, then maybe visit Katrina. Or maybe Aurora would wander town aimlessly until she found an aim.

Snowy was right on Aurora's heels as Aurora held open *Apples Cores'* main doors. Maybe Aurora opened the door a bit too carelessly, since it smacked someone in the face. Someone standing behind the door and giving a few cents to a street artist playing paint-can-drums on the sidewalk.

"Ouch," the man behind the door said.

Aurora recognized the voice and winced. "Max?" She let the door close and stepped around Snowy.

Max was still rubbing his forehead as he smiled and said, "Oh. Hi, Aurora." He closed his wallet and opened the door to *Apples Cores;* they both headed in to take a seat and order.

Max petted Snowy and ordered two ginger teas.

Aurora chuckled to herself. "Just like your hair."

Max shrugged. "What are you doing around this part of town?" he asked.

"Wandering."

Max nodded slowly, and proceeded to answer his own question. "I'm looking to see whether Dr. Doktor will employ me as a psychologist. I'm not sure where the clinic is, though, since she moves the location frequently."

The tea arrived and Aurora took a sip, burning the tip of her tongue. "It's very hot," she noted.

"That's how they make tea, if I understand correctly."

Aurora shrugged, then told Max that her birthday was coming up on Saturday. "I'm going to have a party tomorrow at home. Do you want to come?"

"Yes." Max answered quickly. He repeated, with more poise, "I mean, I'd love to!"

There was a moment of awkward silence.

Then, Snowy brushed past Max's leg, and Max petted Snowy. "Snowy is such a good cat," he said.

Aurora rolled her eyes and told Max about the previous night, and all the weeks before. "Snowy always comes back, though, within a few hours. I don't know where she's going - probably to sulk around town as cats do?"

"I've heard of similar stories," Max told her. "Back when I worked for Dr. Doktor as a veterinarian receptionist on a psychology internship, quite a few cat owners mentioned that their cats disappeared regularly. It's probably nothing, and I'm sure it happens to all cat owners at some point."

Aurora thought about this. The tea seemed to be getting cold. Aurora sipped her tea.

"I can even give you some of their contacts," Max said, starting to write down some numbers on a napkin. "If you feel like investigating the 'Missing Cats of Verwood.'"

Aurora tucked the numbers into her coat pocket and thanked Max.

As she got up, Max also palmed her a bar of chocolate. "I bought too many," he admitted shyly. "Anyways, have a nice day, Aurora. See you tomorrow night."

Aurora smiled to herself, and tried to stop blushing, but she couldn't. For the whole walk home.

Back in her apartment, she finally read the ingredients on the chocolate cover, and set the chocolate in the fridge so it wouldn't melt. She started setting up for her party the following day.

Chapter 2

After hanging four streamers on a window, Aurora gave up and laid down on her couch, only to find that something was poking her back. It was her phone, still inside her jacket. Aurora took out her phone to check for any messages, and then emptied the rest of her coat's pocket.

The grand total amounted to: four bobby pins, a toy car, two purple-ink pens, her voice recorder pen, a business card from Dr. Doktor, and the napkin Max gave her.

Aurora sat up with a new interest and rewrote the phone numbers on a clean sheet of paper. She began to dial them up. The first two numbers didn't pick up the phone, but the third did.

"Hello? This is Aurora Frost, Private Investigator, I'm currently working on a case about missing cats. I've heard from a friend that you've mentioned your cat going missing."

On the other end was an old woman. Her voice was shaky. "Pillow - my cat - still goes missing. Yesterday night he was gone for two hours."

Aurora took notes on the rest of the conversation, and then wished the old woman a good day and cut the line. There were four more numbers, and they all picked up the call. All of them said similar things: their cats had been going missing for the past few months, almost 5 months in one case. The disappearances were usually around midnight.

Most of the cat-owners didn't have the best memory, but upon Aurora's suggestion that the disappearances happened on a specific day, all of them said Thursday.

Only one of the owners seemed to have a slightly different case. "You have two cats?" Aurora asked over the phone.

"Yes. Linky and Jinky."

"And only *one* goes missing every Thursday?"

"Yes, but Jinky is bedridden."

"What about Linky?" Aurora asked.

"Linky is very sad that Jinky is bedridden."

"Oh. That's… that's too bad. I meant to ask how Linky was doing regarding, umm... about the Thursday midnight outings?"

"Ah, that. Linky comes back happy every night. Very calm, with no worries."

She bid farewell and set down the phone. The notes seemed to indicate the same that Aurora had suspected all along. There were many cats, all going missing every Thursday night for a few hours. All the owners had no idea where their cats were going.

Evidently, this was a bigger problem than Snowy. Aurora was now on a case!

Chapter 3

It was Saturday, Aurora's birthday. If birthdays were still working the same way they did last year, then she was turning one year older!

She was a bit sad that Natalia and Aleks could not attend: Aurora had called earlier and Natalia had answered the phone. Apparently they had arranged for a visit to Viola on the same day, and they could not cancel.

"Come by anytime after you get back," Aurora had told Natalia.

"We will! Have a happy birthday, Aurora!" Natalia had ended the call.

Presently, Aurora was recalling memory fragments from the past few days. There was no reason to be nervous, but Aurora was. There was a curiously nervous quality about waiting, whether it was for news, results, or guests. Aurora was waiting for the latter when her phone rang.

She picked it up and held it to her ear, only to hear two familiar voices say "Happy birthday, Aurora!!" slightly out of sync.

"Mom? Dad?" Aurora asked.

There was a slight pause, and wind whistled on the other end. Then, a crackle. "Yes, it's us!"

Aurora was crying tears of happiness as she said, "I - how have you both been?"

The phone cut out for two minutes before it connected again and her parents said, "We're doing fine."

"Just remember," added her mother, "the motto: However lost you are, stay cool."

And, Aurora was definitely staying cool as she wiped away superfluous tears and said, "I miss you both! When will you be visiting back?"

Her parents told her a date, to which Aurora argued they should come earlier, to which her parents cited names and health conditions of various penguins. Eventually, conversation turned to Aurora's most recent adventures, and Aurora excitedly narrated each detail over the line. Aurora especially described her visit to the museum in great detail, in memory of her frequent visits there as a child.

Finally, the connection became more spotted, and Aurora told her parents "Call again soon" before setting the phone back on the receiver. She began to sort through her mail, and found a few advertisements for seemingly ineffective stress therapy programs.

At the bottom of the pile was an envelope from Antarctica, and Aurora knew what she was looking at even before she opened it. It was a nice picture of Aurora's parents in Antarctica wearing furry coats and surrounded by fluffy penguins. And right behind it was a picture of Aurora and her parents at the *South Pole* special exhibition at the museum.

She was looking at every detail of the photo carefully, and she was startled when her doorbell rang at 4:00PM.

On the other side of the door was Max. He held a little present box. He peeked into the apartment and noticed he was the first guest to arrive. "I hope I'm not too early."

Aurora shook her head and confirmed that he wasn't, even though he was. They both sat in the main room, and Aurora adjusted the decorations a bit more.

"Here's a present for Snowy," Max said, handing her the small box.

Aurora opened the box and wondered why Max would get Snowy a present on Aurora's birthday. Inside was a little bell.

"To track when Snowy jumps out the window and maybe follow her," Max explained.

Aurora tied it on Snowy's collar and smiled to herself. Max was so thoughtful…

The doorbell rang. Katrina Mousey Bumbly, Jerry Mousey Bumbly, and Shaggy-Dog Mousey Bumbly all came in.

"Oh, I know you," Katrina said to Max immediately. "You're the one who helped Shaggy-Dog with the…" Then, Katrina spotted Aurora, her best friend, and they shared a long hug. "Happy birthday!!!!"

They spent hours talking, and ate the cupcakes. Katrina, Jerry, and Shaggy-Dog had to leave by 7:00PM for another event.

Aurora and Max spend the next half hour chatting about the disappearing cats in Verwood. Eventually Max suggested they eat popsicles, and Aurora told him it was in the freezer, above the fridge. She was tightening the bell on Snowy's neck when Max came back.

He was quiet as he leaned against the dividing wall between the two rooms. He watched Aurora until she looked up at him.

"Did I run out of popsicles?" Aurora asked him.

He shook his head, *no*. After a second, "The chocolate I gave you was in the fridge, though."

"It melts if I leave it out," Aurora said matter-of-factly. "I'm not in a very chocolatey mood today."

"We can split it," he suggested.

"No, that's fine," she said. When she noticed the look of dismay on Max's face, she added, "But I like…"

Max seemed frozen in anticipation.

"I liked the… umm… thought behind the gift very much," Aurora sputtered. "I'll eat it tomorrow." She mentally slapped herself for always saying the most awkward things. *Especially* with Max around.

Max, however, didn't seem to notice. "Thanks," he said, handing her an orange flavored, orange colored popsicle which sat firmly on an orange stick.

Aurora asked Max when his birthday was.

"Oh, I'm not really sure," said Max.

Aurora looked at him. "You don't know your birthday?"

Max shook his head. "That's the thing about being born on a farm, they just don't write things down unless they find paper."

Aurora realized that Lance had mentioned this many months ago as well. The rural people around Verwood had a strange habit of only writing things on paper if they could find paper and a writing utensil in the moment. If not written, it was simply forgotten. That was the explanation for many rural phenomena like people not knowing the date, and shoppers unsure of how many pomegranates they needed to purchase. Truly, these were the reasons why paper sold so terribly out in the rural areas, because it was regarded as a nice-to-have rather than a necessity.

"So, you don't know your birthday?" Aurora repeated to Max.

"But I know the year I was born, because this tree was felled in the same year and they wrote down that date somewhere."

Aurora nodded slowly, finishing her popsicle. "So what about your parents?"

"What about them?"

"I don't know, what about them?"

Max seemed guarded when he related anything to his past. He said after a long pause, "They still live on the same farm where I grew up. They still think paper is a nice-to-have. You know, the usual."

He checked his watch and informed Aurora that he had to go downtown for a meeting with Dr. Doktor. After kissing the back of her hand, he wished her a great day.

The moment Aurora closed the door behind Max, she frustratedly sat down on her couch and wondered why Max was so guarded about his past. *What was going on there?* He was so kind and gentle, but this part of him was the most curious thing she had ever happened upon. At first she wondered why she couldn't admit to Max that she maybe, a little bit, *liked him,* and now Aurora was left wondering who Max really was.

Her thoughts were interrupted by a quick rap on the door, and this time Aurora opened it to find a small gift. Maybe three inches cubed, she estimated, thanking that course on *Estimating Sizes of Boxes* she'd taken in her free period during middle school. She used a nearby ruler to measure the box, and confirmed its size at three inches cubed.

The box was wrapped in shiny orange paper, with a note signed by *Caroit Green.*

Aurora peeked both ways down the hallway, yet no one was present. She shut the door and returned to her couch, unwrapping her present slowly. She got through the first layer of wrapping paper when her Aunt Cassia called.

"Happy Birthday, Aurora," Cassia said.

Aurora, eyeing the half-opened gift from Caroit on her table, asked her Aunt if anything notable had happened recently in Viola.

"It's a quiet town, you know?" Cassia said.

"I'm investigating Snowy's disappearances," Aurora told her aunt.

"Well, be careful. If you're wandering town at midnight, make sure you take someone with you."

Aurora agreed and set the phone back on the receiver. The crime rates in Verwood were at an all time low due to

Aurora's exemplary detective skills, but she knew that the city was still dangerous. She wrote a reminder-note to ask someone to come with her at midnight, set it on the table, and lost it promptly.

Her birthday was no time to be sorry for losing a note, she told herself, and turned back to Caroit's gift instead.

The rest of the giftwrap on the gift tore off quickly to reveal a little bag and a pen. The bag had a tiny magnifying glass in it, with "Aurora" carved on the handle. And the pen, engraved "VPD" for the Verwood Police Department, had a flashlight and two lockpicks hidden inside of it.

Aurora placed the magnifying glass on her mantel and pocketed the pen. She sent a quick voicemail to Caroit expressing her gratitude.

The rest of the evening she spent on her own. It was calm and quiet, and she petted Snowy gingerly before going to sleep. Even Snowy seemed to wish Aurora a happy birthday with a quiet "meow."

Chapter 4

It was Thursday once again. The day after Wednesday. The day before Friday. There was an air of excitement, of suspense, and of boredom.

Snowy was angrily pawing at her bell, as she had been doing the whole week.

Aurora's plan was to follow Snowy out the window and into the city, so she slept dressed in warm jeans and a sweater. She kept her coat by her bed. She pretended to sleep around 11:00 PM, and within minutes, Snowy's bell indicated that the cat had left the bedroom.

Aurora rushed out, and climbed through the kitchen window, onto the fire escape. It was a bit shaky, so Aurora was thankful that there were only three floors to descend. Snowy seemed to slow down and lick herself, but then jumped down the next few floors. Aurora pursued, jumping down the last few steps with her eyes fixed on Snowy. Max's bell helped.

On the sidewalk, Aurora noticed a shadowy figure leaning against the brick wall, and tried her best to walk around, but they seemed to follow her. Aurora quickened her pace.

"Aurora, are you following your cat?" the shadowy figure's voice asked. It was Aleks!

Aurora turned around enough to confirm that it was Aleks, then proceeded to follow Snowy, who seemed to have slowed down. "Aleks, are you following *me*?" Aurora mimicked.

"I'm on my midnight walk!" Aleks said in defense.

"Who goes for midnight walks around the city? Plus, Detective Aeyto's house is on the other side of the city!" Aurora glanced back to ensure Aleks was still following her. She was oddly comforted knowing that he was with her, and that she wasn't all alone. For a moment, Aurora wondered if her Aunt Cassia had set up Aleks on this mission as a protective accompaniment.

Aurora decided against it - Aleks would never follow someone else's instructions. Besides, he was too happy to have been following Aurora on Aunt Cassia's order.

He occasionally tapped Aurora's shoulder to ensure that she was right in front of him, and it soon turned into a mini tag-game between the two of them. Aurora tapped Aleks' shoulder, then Aleks tapped Aurora's, and so on and so forth.

There was giggling involved, yet Snowy didn't seem to notice them at all. It was definitely odd behavior.

Before they knew it, they needed to turn a corner. The alley before them was dark. Aurora pulled out her new VPD flashlight-pen and shined it in front of her. It wasn't the brightest, but Aurora supposed it would have to do.

As her eyes adjusted to the dark, she noticed a mountain of cardboard boxes blocking the way. Aleks had already begun to unstack a few.

"It's really dark, and there might be rats in the boxes," Aurora noted.

Aleks laughed and moved to the left side of the alleyway, then without looking flipped on a hidden switch. Decorative lines of lights turned on above them: white, blue and purple.

"How did you know about the lights?" Aurora asked.

"Someone told me," he said vaguely. "Here, put this box over there."

"Who told you?"

"A friend."

"Which friend?" Aurora pressed.

Aleks paused and leaned on a wall. "Aurora, when have I ever done anything through conventional means?"

Aurora muttered *"touché"* and helped Aleks move the boxes aside. She couldn't help but wonder who his friend was. *Was this why she wasn't seeing Aleks around as much as she used to?* Aurora shook away the thought: he was strolling through her neighborhood at midnight. This friend was no competition for Aurora - none at all.

Aurora cringed at her confidence, and looked back to the mountain of boxes ahead.

The quickest way to get across this row of buildings was through this alley, but evidently Thursday was "Cardboard Club" night. According to a nearby poster, everyone in Verwood was encouraged to recycle cardboard on Thursday nights, and place it in *this* alley.

Aurora could still hear Snowy's bell not too far away. After Aurora and Aleks had managed to move twenty boxes, Aurora climbed up a box and could spot Snowy sitting a few feet away.

She felt Aleks' hand grasp hers. "Come on!" he called. Somehow he'd climbed ahead of her, and was standing on the "peak" of the cardboard-box mountain.

Aurora reached for his hand, and he pulled her up. They descended the other side together, still holding hands, only to find Snowy had crossed the road.

"The crosswalk is that way," Aurora said, pointing left.

"It's only four lanes, and no one is on them," Aleks argued, pulling Aurora along.

Aurora almost scolded Aleks, but the freedom of running across the empty main road at night made her feel, well, free. *Aleks can be annoying, but he's definitely daring. And only with the best intentions for me.* Even though Aleks and Snowy were perfect enemies, Aleks strived to reunite Aurora with her cat - something which made Aurora tighten her grasp on Aleks' hand even more.

He didn't seem to notice, and instead pointed out the large arch above them. According to the words on the arch, they were in front of the Verwood Central Park's main entrance.

Chapter 5

"The park?" Aurora asked, baffled. "Snowy sneaks away to go to the *park* every Thursday night?"

"You don't take Snowy to the park often enough," Aleks joked.

Aurora stuck out her tongue. She started down the pathway and heard a faint whirring sound. Aurora peeked over the shrubbery to her right upon instinct and spotted a wide circle of 13 cats.

"Cats," Aleks muttered.

They were equally spaced, and a robed man in the middle held a wand with swirls. He seemed to be hypnotizing the cats.

"I need a closer look," Aurora told Aleks.

But Aleks' grip on Aurora's wrist tightened. He pulled out a small camera and set it on the top of the shrubbery. It recorded the event, but the image seemed blurry. "The lighting is bad," Aleks explained.

"So I'll go closer and investigate," Aurora argued.

Aleks simply looked into Aurora's eyes for a minute. There was an intensity in his gaze which Aurora could not argue with, and her urge to investigate faded.

"Fine, I'll stay," she said. Perhaps she spoke too loudly, for Snowy's ears perked up.

Snowy shook herself out of the hypnosis and crawled towards where Aurora and Aleks were hiding. Snowy crawled around the shrubbery and then looked between Aurora and Aleks. Snowy proceeded to scratch at Aleks' legs.

"Ouch!" Aleks said as quietly as he could. He picked up Snowy and ruffled the cat's head gingerly. He looked at Aurora protectively. "Well, we've investigated enough for tonight, Aurora. Ready to head home?"

But Aurora had already managed her way around the shrubbery wall and began to approach the hypnotic man.

The Arrest

Aurora decided that this hypnotic man could not have been that dangerous. He was shorter than Aurora - which meant shorter than five-foot-three - and he wore thick glasses. He broke the hypnosis with the remaining twelve cats, who all started their way back home.

He turned to Aurora. He had trouble walking towards her, since he kept tripping on his robe.

"What is this?" Aurora asked.

The man looked at Aurora for a moment, then asked, "Is the fluffy white one your cat?"

Aurora nodded. "I'm a private investigator here, and I would like to know what you're doing with all these cats. Every Thursday."

The man straightened his glasses, then gestured to a nearby bench. Aurora glanced at Aleks, still hidden behind the shrubbery, before taking a seat.

"Explain," Aurora prompted.

"I invite cats here by reaching out in a different plane. I hypnotize the cats to take away their stress. I wanted to run clinical trials, but no one gives me funding, so I lure 13 cats out here every Thursday night to run a hypnotic test. I keep amending the exact treatment I give every week to improve the stress reduction in each cat." He paused.

Aurora remembered Linky the cat, who was happier after its nightly adventure. Even Snowy was notably less stressed every Friday morning when Aurora came to think about it.

"I'm doing these trials with the belief that, someday, this hypnosis will be able to cure many diseases in humans as well. For the good of humanity."

Aurora didn't know what to say.

"For the good of humanity," he repeated.

"I… I understand," Aurora started, "but you can't take cats without permission. Or any living creature. Or dead creatures, for that matter. No more taking without permission."

"I won't anymore, I promise." He added, sternly, "But I need to continue these tests to improve my method."

There was a pause. "Now, I'm supposed to call the police to arrest you," Aurora told him strictly. "If you promise not to… to lure, abduct, and hypnotize cats anymore, then maybe I'll let you free, since no harm was done. Promise?"

The man stood quietly. There was a rough gust of wind, and Aurora pulled her coat tighter.

In the silence, she fished around in her coat pocket for a familiar business card. "Here's the contact information for a local veterinarian, Dr. Doktor. A friend of mine works at the clinic now, and may be able to help you get cats for your experiments in more… more legal ways."

The man plucked the card from Aurora's hand and skimmed it. He pushed his round glasses up his nose, then said, "I promise. No more trials without permission. No more Trial Thursdays." He stumbled off into the night, tripping on his robe.

Aurora, still sitting, turned around in her seat to notice Snowy at her ankles. Aleks was leaning against the back of a bench right behind her.

"That man was odd," Aleks said.

"Agreed. But I recorded our conversation and you took a video of him, right? For proof?" Aurora asked.

Aleks nodded and handed her the camera. With a grin, he added, "And… look at this…"

Aurora took the camera and peered at the little box where the photos would show up. The little icon at the top indicated the camera was in front-facing mode. Aleks was leaning over the park bench so his head appeared right above Aurora's in the little frame-preview screen.

The big number on the screen was a countdown! It was at "1," and before Aurora could pause it, the shutter flashed and then Aleks took the camera back.

Aurora grinned at Aleks's brilliant move, but he wasn't looking at her, instead intensely peering down the park's walkway. *He was looking to make sure the path back was clear,* Aurora realized. It made her melt a little inside.

"Time to go back home," Aleks told Aurora, taking her hand in his. They walked back to Verwood Grove Apartments together.

As they reached the building, Aurora felt a bit sad inside. They only had a few more steps to go: turn a corner and they'd be in the downstairs lobby of her apartment building where they'd have to part ways.

But instead of continuing their path around the building, Aleks stopped. "Not the elevator, please," Aleks requested jokingly, bringing a smile back to Aurora's face. They took the fire escape up to the third floor, and the brick facade only snagged on Aurora's jacket twice. Aleks was there both times to un-snag it.

Aurora pushed up the window enough to let Snowy in, and pulled herself onto the windowsill with Aleks' help. The wind was chilly as it blew through her hair, and the stars were bright above. She paused to sit on the windowsill because she didn't want the night to end - not yet.

She felt Alek's hand in her palm, and looked down. "The video proof, on a flash drive," Aleks explained. "And the photo of both of us. Consider it a bonus."

Aurora paused for a moment, not wanting to break the moment.

"Is that all?" Aleks asked, nervously. "Need anything else?"

"No, this is perfect." With a wide smile, Aurora added, "Good night, Aleks."

"Good night, Aurora. And happy belated birthday."

24

Fear of Blue Colored Pencils

Wearing a hat

Got into a spat

Hospital bed

Patient files read

Aurora knows who

Prologue

Aurora's mind was filled with thoughts as she drove back home. It was filled with thoughts of her friend, Katrina Mousey Bumbly, whose house she'd visited. Natalia had gone there to discuss the next play Katrina would write, and Aleks had followed his sister. Aurora ended up getting a call around ten in the morning, from Katrina, who said Aurora should come, and bring Snowy too.

So, Aurora had gone, and there was nothing particularly interesting at Katrina's house. It was pink as it had always been as she'd pulled up onto Katrina's driveway. She spent lunch at Katrina's house, and for most of her four hours there, she chatted with Aleks regarding something or the other. It had been a few weeks since they'd last met, and Aleks had numerous exciting stories to tell. She enjoyed her time with them, and had forgotten how annoyingly sarcastic Aleks could be. She didn't exactly dislike it, either.

Back on the road, Aurora focused on the stoplight, willing it to turn green. She had the worst luck, it seemed, as she missed every green light on her way back. Snowy pawed at the car's dashboard, at a packet of cat treats.

"You want more treats?" Aurora asked.

Snowy meowed.

"Okay, we can go to the speciality shop then." Aurora kept driving straight instead of taking a right, and soon arrived at the Verwood Gift Shop, which was adjacent to the Verwood Hospital. The gift shop was for tourists and specialty goods alike. Parking was scarce, so Aurora had to park in the street right outside the shop.

As she wandered in, the door's bells jingled. Snowy trailed behind her, pawing at each treat that was of interest.

"Only two packets," Aurora told Snowy, leaving her cat to shop for herself. Snowy browsed the aisles and began dragging packets to make a pile. Meanwhile, Aurora browsed the higher shelves, filled with little yarn dolls, boxes of assorted feathers - purple, black, pastel yellow - and paper-flower bouquets.

Snowy poked at Aurora's ankles, so she followed her cat and picked up the two packets of cat treats. Aurora, now energetic from driving around town, dreaded going back to her home, and wondered whether she'd have the time to go back to Katrina's house.

The Featherman

In the Pediatric ICU of Verwood's hospital, there were four rooms. They were mostly empty, but for the two beds in each. Only one room was currently occupied.

Calvin, one of the patients, traced his name card, which sat on the little table next to his bed. Calvin was eight years old, liked to tell stories, and had only one leg. He slept most of the time, but when he was awake, he'd talk excitedly about the things he'd seen in his dreams.

The audience for most of his stories was his roommate, Claire. Claire had some sort of problem, the doctors said, but Calvin liked to imagine that Claire's needle - inserted in her arm - gave her special listening skills. Claire had been in the ICU when Calvin moved in, and she had turned seven years old the previous week.

She could not hear, nor speak, said the doctors. The doctors said Claire had learned the art of nodding along whenever Calvin was talking. Calvin believed that they were lying and that Claire did, in fact, hear his stories.

Claire shook a paper in front of Calvin, moving the boy from his deep thoughts.

"What's it say?" Calvin asked, reaching over. Claire hadn't been able to draw or write well ever since "the incident." Calvin had yet to pick up the details of "the incident," but he knew it took place because the people in white coats talked about it often.

The paper Claire had handed Calvin, however, had a few squiggles on it. It was of two friends, like the two of them, playing in a grassy field. Calvin could also distinguish a rainbow in the background, and birds with long black feathers. "I like the drawing," Calvin told her, before launching into a long explanation of what she should draw next.

By the time he'd finished, it was night, and the lights in the hospital turned off with a click.

Calvin fell into a light sleep promptly, but in the middle of the night, he heard sounds. He sat up in his bed and looked around.

Nothing was there, except for a friendly lamp, which seemed to wave hello to him.

So he laid back down and, after saying good night to the lamp, fell asleep once again.

But there was another sound. It happened a few hours after the first. The sound was of the door to the room opening and closing.

Calvin opened his eyes surreptitiously and looked around. There was a long shadow against the door, created by the happily waving lamp.

A tall man created the shadow. And he was approaching Claire cautiously. He pulled out the needle from Claire's arm, which fell to the ground with a quiet clatter.

As he turned to leave, the shadow grew shorter, and the little black feather in his hat seemed to cackle.

Chapter 1

Aurora was not a reckless driver, which is why it surprised her when she almost drove into someone as she made a u-turn at the end of the shops' street downtown. She hit the brakes immediately, and thankfully both Aurora and Snowy were buckled into their seats, so they didn't get hurt.

However, the young man who'd fallen off his bicycle seemed to have a few scrapes on his knees. Aurora recognized him instantly, and parked the car nearby in the hospital parking lot. She felt bad and hoped he was fine.

"I'm fine," Max told Aurora as she jogged back to him.

"Are you sure?" Aurora asked.

Max had parked his bike a few feet away and was sitting on the curb a few yards away from where Aurora had nearly run into him. He had a small cardboard box next to him as well, filled with what looked like greeting cards. Running a hand through his hair, he said, looking away from Aurora, "Yes, I'm completely fine."

"Why, umm, do you bike?"

"Oh, I used to bike all the time back on the farm back home." Max seemed more open this time when he mentioned his farm back home. But Aurora still wondered…

Aurora fiddled with her fingers. Luckily, Snowy broke the silence when she jumped on Max. They seemed equally excited to see each other, and Snowy leaned into a few strokes on her head..

Finally Max said, "I'm going to drop off cards to kids and elderly patients at the hospital."

That's what the "get well" cards were for. Aurora picked up the box. "It seems I'll be joining you then."

Max smiled.

Aurora took it as a cue to start walking towards the hospital's main entrance. Max got up a few seconds later and jogged to catch up.

"How has the detective business been?" Max asked Aurora.

Aurora realized she hadn't spoken to Max since her birthday, and an awkward silence held taut between them. Carrot had given her a few case files to thumb through, but she hadn't done any exciting field work recently. She said so to Max.

"Too bad," he said. "I come by the hospital every few weeks to drop off greeting cards, and meet patients. Apparently it's good training for a psychologist to be around people in distress, so…"

"… you're in training," Aurora finished.

"Exactly." He politely held open the door and the elevator, and showed Aurora the way to the long-term wing of the Verwood Hospital.

Aurora realized she'd missed this - Max's politeness - as she set the box of cards down on a reception desk.

"I'm going to take a few upstairs to the older patients, but there are two really sweet kids in room 24," Max told Aurora.

"Room 24?" Aurora asked.

"Yeah, I'll meet you there," Max said, leaning behind Aurora to grab a smaller box out of the cardboard box. Their shoulders brushed lightly.

Aurora watched Max walk towards the elevator before lifting the box. Within seconds, she got lost on the sprawling floor, and after Snowy scratched at her legs a few times, Aurora decided to ask for assistance. "Room 24? I'm supposed to meet two kids there," Aurora said.

The man at the front desk was buried in papers and when he looked up, a few papers fell to the ground. "24? The girl is in the emergency room right now, because her needle fell out last night, but the boy should be in. It's down the hall, two rights, a left, a u-turn, and two more lefts."

Aurora thanked him and followed the odd instructions. She reached the room in no time, and when she opened the door, she saw a young boy sleeping.

The name tag near his bed said "Calvin."

Aurora set the box of cards on the ground and Snowy pawed at them while Aurora awkwardly stood, hands in her deep coat pockets. She tapped her foot quietly for five minutes, then tried undoing a knot she subconsciously tied into her scarlet-bead bracelet in the previous five minutes.

She failed in that effort, and signed loudly.

The sleeping boy started to mumble. "No, I don't want that dinosaur, I want the one with the feathers."

Aurora tried to listen closely, but the boy stopped talking, so she continued to watch the analog clock on the wall tick. Twelve more minutes passed when Max sauntered in, with an adhesive bandage across one knee. He took in the situation quickly.

"Sorry to leave you waiting," he apologized.

"No, no problem, I mean..." Aurora shrugged.

"Okay."

"How were the other patients?"

"Good." Max said.

"... Good."

Max nodded as if Aurora had asked a question. Then, "Has he said anything?"

Aurora blinked twice. "Who?"

"Calvin."

"Something about dinosaurs and feathers. It comprised the most entertaining ten seconds of the past twenty minutes."

Snowy started to wave between Max's legs and after a few seconds of silence, Max blushed in embarrassment. "I guess there isn't much left. I'm going to wait until Calvin wakes up, but - "

"I'm awake," the young boy said without moving.

Aurora and Max turned quickly to face the young boy, who was still sleeping on his side turned away from them.

"Good afternoon," Max said calmly. He looked at Aurora as if something was wrong.

Aurora didn't know what to expect next, but the conversation seemed to continue normally.

"I ate breakfast and told the doctors I saw the featherman last night but they didn't believe me," Calvin said sweetly.

"Who's the featherman?" Max asked.

"The man with the black feather in his hat."

"And he came here last night?"

"That's why they took away Claire, I think."

"They took away Claire because the featherman came here," Max repeated.

"That's what he said," Aurora jumped in. She started to understand that something was off - that something had happened to Claire.

"That's what she said," Calvin said.

Max looked between the Aurora and Calvin. "So there was a featherman?"

Calvin said, "Yes. And he was mean."

"How mean?"

"Very mean. Closer to average than you and me, so very mean."

Max almost slapped his forehead in annoyance of Calvin's statistics joke but refrained from doing so. Aurora suppressed a laugh.

"Describe the featherman," Aurora said, but Max intervened.

"I think this is enough story time. Now, tell me what you ate for breakfast." Max smiled since Calvin was frowning at him.

Aurora grabbed Max's arm and turned him to face the door, away from Calvin. "I think he's giving us clues," she told Max.

"Calvin is… he has a great imagination. A really vivid imagination. I think he's missing his friend," Max argued.

Aurora sighed. "But he was talking about feathers in his *dream*. Subconscious. And the girl's needle *fell out*. Needles don't just fall out."

"We shouldn't stress him out."

"I'm not stressed out," Calvin said from across the room. "Mr. Roosters, you and your girlfriend whisper louder than the featherman."

Aurora's face went redder than Max's hair.

And, this time Max actually face-palmed. "Don't worry about the featherman," he assured Calvin, placing a bouquet and toy car on his table. They had been, somehow, hidden in the box of get-well cards.

Max took Aurora's hand and led her and Snowy (still walking around Max's feet) outside.

Chapter 2

"Carrot says this is all speculation. He says we need proof and I agree," Aurora told Max. She had just spent a half hour on the phone with Detective Caroit Green of the Verwood Police Department. Aurora was a Private Investigator, and worked on official cases, sometimes officially, sometimes not. So, she often had to report back to Caroit, or Carrot as she referred to him. "We need to talk to Calvin for more proof," Aurora insisted.

"I talked to the front office staff, who said needles don't fall out like this often." Max sighed, "I guess you were right. I'm going back in to talk to Calvin."

"We."

"Fine, but you can't talk. You might stress him out."

"And you won't?"

Max gave Aurora a look.

"You know what to ask him? Exactly what to ask him?" Aurora asked.

Max grinned, with no verbal answer. Aurora took it as a *yes*.

The two, plus Snowy, entered Calvin's hospital room once more.

"Hi cat," Calvin said quickly. He was now sitting, blanket over his leg. He waved happily.

Max sat down on the edge of Claire's empty bed.

Calvin happily pointed that out. And the piece of paper under Max's shoe.

"Now, do you remember what happened last night?" Max prompted.

"I was sleeping."

"And then?"

"I slept more."

Aurora and Max exchanged a look. "Does 'featherman' mean anything to you?" Max asked.

"He visited Claire."

"And?"

"Pulled the needle out of her hand."

"Describe him if you can remember," Max specified.

"Well, he was in the dark, so I can't say exactly." Calvin went silent for a moment before his eyes suddenly lit up. "I want four more toy cars if I tell you."

"Okay," Aurora interceded, and pulled out a few models she found in the depths of her coat pockets. She placed two on Calvin's stand and held onto the others. "Tell us everything you know, and you get the others."

"Bribery is not - " Max started. He sighed when both Aurora and Calvin frowned at him. "Fine, describe the featherman."

Calvin looked between them both ominously. "The door opened very, very slowly, and the lamp was waving at me. The door closed. *BLAM*. And the featherman had a feather, dark black, in his hat."

"And?" Max asked.

"That's all," Calvin said cheerfully. He laid down again and promptly slept. Aurora left the other two cars on Calvin's table.

Aurora and Max once again retreated to the hallway outside Calvin's room. Snowy laid down against the wall. Aurora and Max talked about the new information they'd gathered, which was practically nothing.

"But the conviction with which he repeated the information leads me to think there's some truth in it," Max noted.

Aurora smiled, holding up an orchid-colored voice recorder. "Good thing I recorded it!"

Chapter 3

"You're the *bakawk* detective girl," identified Verwood Hospital's neurosurgeon. She was technically on break since no one had brain problems, or so she claimed, since she was sitting in a waiting area of the Verwood Hospital. She had on her lap a few magazines about chicken-work on clothing, and seemed to have completed them.

Aurora knew she recognized this woman, and upon reading the nametag, knew instantly from where.

"Dr. Doktor. Nice to see you again." Max shook hands with her. "Once again, thank you so much for allowing me to be an intern at your veterinarian clinic. It was an invaluable experience."

"My honor," Dr. Doktor said.

Aurora had forgotten they knew each other, but figured it made sense that Max, a student of psychology, would have met the exemplary, multi-disciplinary Dr. Nerz Doktor.

Max and Aurora asked to see the security cameras. Dr. Doktor took them to a backroom, large and spacious, with monitors installed on every surface, including the ceiling and floor. And the door. Snowy was too scared, so she stayed outside in the hallway.

"Which one is room 24?" Aurora asked.

Dr. Doktor pointed out a small monitor on a table in the corner, with boxes of hundreds of USB drives containing the recordings of recent events. She left them to investigate. "Good *bakawk* luck," she said as she shut the door.

"Divide and conquer?" Max suggested.

They went through all the drives in the box labeled room 24, and collected a pile of everything between 5PM to 9AM. And they watched them all on fast forward while sitting on separate swiveling chairs.

It didn't help them one bit since it was all erased, or corrupted. There was a single picture of a crow pasted over the actual recording, and that picture ran over the video for the entire 14 hours.

Finally, Aurora mentioned to Max that at least the black feather was confirmed.

"With no proof other than a kid's blabberings and this picture of a - of a constipated crow!" Max shouted. He ran a hand through his hair. "Sorry for being so... so frustrated. So upset."

Aurora didn't know what to say, since she had never seen him so frustrated in the past. *The past*... Aurora wondered what Max used to be like, if that was anything different, even. Was he frustrated like this all the time? What inspired him to study psychology, *truly*?

Aurora pulled herself back to the present. After weighing the pros and cons of a few options, she decided to pat his shoulder slowly. Max laid his head on her hand, and suddenly she became aware that they were the only two people in the room. She wondered what would happen next, both scared and excited. A bit thrilled.

Max turned to face her, still having his head on her shoulder. His hair was soft.

Aurora froze, unsure what to do or say.

"The crow looks quite creepy. Want to head out for a snack somewhere?" Max suggested.

Aurora nodded quickly. And then hoped she didn't seem too desperate, or anything.

"Would you like a pretzel, or anything?" There was a young cashier boy behind the billing counter at the snack section. He was very seriously typing in the costs, poking the calculator's "equals" button every other second. He straightened his little baseball cap so it fit backwards, and then, finishing the billing, handed a receipt to Aurora. "Say hi to my Uncle Caroit for me," he said with a smile.

Aurora winked at him and passed an extra dollar as a tip. "Will do. Hope you enjoy the rest of your summer job!"

As Max and Aurora walked away from the billing counter, Max asked, "Detective Green has a nephew?"

Aurora nodded. "Green Bean is an extremely intelligent kid. Like his uncle, but a million times 'hipper,' according to Green Bean's self report."

They found a seat and sat as Cel Green walked by. Greetings were exchanged, and life lessons told. After an hour of that, Aurora said bye to both Cel and Max, since Snowy's meows urged her to return home.

Evidently, Snowy wanted another snack.

Chapter 4

~~ Harley Darley ~~

"Please don't run away. Read *here* - just stay." Marley left Harley in a corner with some files, since she was called into work unexpectedly. Harley was bored of staying with friends, and his father was still at a hospital near the Smiles and Snuggles Zoo in Australia. So, he accompanied his mother to the Verwood Hospital, where his mother worked as a nurse.

He started to flip through the various files until he saw one with a pair of parallel lines on the top. Harley Darley liked parallel lines because there were two of everything. Two lines, two 180 degree angles. Two directions in which the lines headed endlessly.

He pulled out the file, and it fell to the floor with a "*thud.*"

He pulled in a deep breath and read the file at the speed of light:

> "*Ms. Claire. Six years old.*
> *Admitted for 5 months so far.*
> *Orphan. Admitted after going*
> *deaf during a local explosion*
> *at a bank robbery... She is*
> *possibly the only person who*
> *saw the perpetrator due to her*
> *vantage point. News reports*
> *currently claim the*
> *perpetrator has not been*
> *caught yet. No description has*
> *thus far been given of the*
> *perpetrator.*

> *Progress: Has not yet spoken*
> *or communicated through*
> *alternative methods. Had lost*
> *motor skills like writing at*
> *time of admission, and is*
> *slowly gaining ability to draw*
> *and write once again. The*
> *first occurence of drawing*
> *was during an outdoor*
> *excursion, on mud."*

Stapled to the file were all of Claire's drawings, the top one of which had a rainbow and a black feather on it. Harley Darley ripped the single page off the stack and put it in his pocket.

When Harley Darley put the file away, he got a small papercut on his finger. "Ouch, that's *blood*." He put some clear tape on it, and then walked out against his mother's directions to explore the rest of the hospital.

Chapter 5

Back at home, Aurora watched the news channel. Snowy was in the kitchen trying her snack, which left Aurora free for a few minutes.

The first news story that came up was titled "Another Child With Fear Of Blue Colored Pencils, Cured By Local Prodigy Doctor." It claimed that the fourth child in Verwood was recently cured of this peculiar fear by Dr. Doktor, and played a short clip of the child walking out of the hospital during the night, holding a blue colored pencil. They walked toward the reporter, and proudly showed the camera the pencil.

"I still don't like blue that much, but now I'm not afraid!"

The reporter continued to ask questions in front of the hospital's primary entrance. They asked questions to every single nurse that had ever met with the child, which amounted to a total of fourteen.

Aurora muted the channel and proceeded to fold her laundry, when something in the background of the news clip caught her eye.

There was a tall man in the background, with a feather in his hat.

"Snowy, do you see it too?" she asked, running to set up her camera to record the television. Conveniently, there was a date near the segment title - and it was the same as when Claire's needle had been pulled out.

Aurora stayed quiet and focused on the man in the background. He was at this point quietly leaving the hospital, and Aurora caught a glimpse of the feather in his hat.

"It's him," she said to Snowy, before grabbing her phone and dialing Caroit's number.

As the phone rang, Snowy sauntered into the room and started licking her paws to get the last traces of the snack off. Pieces of the mysterious featherman clicked in Aurora's head, and suddenly she knew where to find the featherman.

"I have some evidence. Meet me in front of the hospital in five minutes," she said to Caroit when he picked up. She added a few details, quickly, then grabbed her bag, her camera, and Snowy. "I'm not sure what the featherman's motive was, but now I can prove that this person exists."

"Meow," Snowy acquiesced as they left the apartment.

The Arrest

This time, Aurora didn't run over Max at the hospital. It was lucky she didn't because she was driving 3.14 miles per hour over the speed limit!

"I think I figured it out," she told Max proudly after finding him chatting with Green Bean in the snack shop.

"Figured out what?" Green Bean asked, adjusting his hat.

"The mystery," Max guessed, smiling proudly as well. He gave Aurora a small hug.

Snowy meowed, and Green Bean rolled his eyes knowingly. "Can I come too?"

The trio and Snowy headed towards the Verwood Gift Shop, where Aurora waved to Caroit as he drove past. After Caroit and Tomato (holding the handcuffs) joined the rest of them, they all stood in silence, looking around themselves for a minute.

"*Vat* are you doing here?" Caroit finally asked when he noticed Green Bean.

Aurora put a finger to her lips. "Waiting for the featherman."

Green Bean excitedly added, "We're doing cool detecting, like detectives do, Uncle Caroit!"

They resumed their quiet stance under the shade of a tree, until another young boy passed them.

"Harley Darley?" Aurora asked, recognizing him.

He handed Aurora a picture. "Thank you for solving my daddy's mystery."

Aurora unfolded it - two kids, a rainbow, and a black feather. The back had:

Patient: Claire | Week 24

written on it. It had been drawn sometime this week! The rest of the group huddled around the drawing to get a closer look.

"Claire's learning to draw," Max noted out loud.

"And she drew a *black feather*. Doesn't that mean something?" Aurora asked. "Harley?" But when she looked up from the drawing, Harley Darley was gone.

The bell on the gift shop's door jingled behind them, and Snowy pawed at Aurora's legs.

Handing the paper to Max, Aurora entered the gift shop quietly. She was determined as she scanned the few aisles. She knew that the door must have been opened by the featherman, because the feather in the perpetrator's hat matched the ones she'd just recently seen sold in the Verwood Gift Shop.

Inside the Verwood Gift Shop, across from her, looking at the handicrafts section, was a tall woman in a black suit.

The featherman was in fact a feather*woman*. She had long black nails, and picked up one black feather- nice and long - from the feather bin. "Just this one," she told the cashier, pulling out the exact number of coins she'd need to pay from a black colored purse.

Aurora was surprised that it was a woman all along. She was staring so hard that she didn't hear when Carrot and Tomato had entered the shop.

She only heard the click of the handcuffs on the featherwoman's wrists.

The feathers woman shook her head quietly and wriggled out of the handcuffs, since her wrists were extremely thin. She had a defiant look in her eyes as she glared at Caroit and stepped on his foot, all the while maintaining eye contact with the tall, lanky detective.

The featherwoman made a dash for it, dropping the coin purse on the ground. Aurora picked up a few coins before they ran too far away and checked the serial number printed on them. "They are sequential," Aurora noted. "I wonder if these were from the recent robbery which occurred about… four or five months ago."

Caroit made note of Aurora's perusal in a small notebook and dropped the coins into a small bag labeled *Exhibit 1*. He skimmed one of the numbers and his eyes widened. "You are right, Aurora." He looked directly at her. "These are the exact serial numbers from that case - I was working on that case earlier this week and remembered the numbers!"

Meanwhile, Snowy jumped off the entrance door frame and landed on the featherwoman's hat. "Ugh, get off of me, you cat," the featherwoman grumbled, trying to regain her poised stature while simultaneously waving her arms in the air trying to detach Snowy from her hat.

While the featherwoman was detained by Snowy's chaotic meowing, Tomato pulled out a belt of ten handcuffs - each a different size. Green Bean, who was patiently working with Detectives Caroit and Tom, used a small ruler to check which would best fit the featherwoman.

"Stay still," Green Bean chided the featherwoman as he measured her wrists as well. He settled on the correctly-sized handcuff and Tomato locked it on the featherwoman's wrists tightly.

"Good work," Caroit said, patting his nephew on the back proudly. As Caroit followed Tomato and the featherwoman, and led Green Bean out, he gave a curt nod to Aurora as he left. Aurora stopped Caroit outside the shop and related the remainder of the details she knew to Caroit, and handed him the camera containing the recording of the featherman leaving the hospital.

"I will visit the hospital for more high-clearance files - it might give us more details on possible motives," Caroit said.

After writing down some more specific locations where information could be found, Aurora bid him goodbye for the day. "If you need anything else, you know where to find me," Aurora said. She returned to the shop and found Max presenting Snowy a small toy. Snowy seemed to love it, but...

For some reason, Aurora wondered why Max wouldn't buy *her* something.

"Snowy has enough toys," Aurora told Max impulsively, looking down.

Max, kneeling by Snowy, looked up. "But look, isn't this so cute? It's a red herring!"

Aurora couldn't help but smile at that, so she said thanks.

~~~~~

Aurora and Max returned to the hospital and were overjoyed to see Claire back in the room with Calvin.

"Did you catch the featherman?" Calvin asked immediately.

"Yes we did!" Aurora said, handing him one of the toy cars she'd found in a box outside their room in the hallway. Then she turned to the girl, who must have been Claire. Claire was watching Aurora very intently with wide eyes.

Aurora took out a black crayon and a fresh piece of paper and drew a feather. Aurora showed the paper to Claire, and the girl clapped.

Beside it, Max took a green crayon and drew a check mark. "We caught the featherwoman," he said, knowing very well Claire couldn't hear it. "She robbed a bank and... of all places, we caught her at a gift shop!"

"We make a great team," Aurora said with a smile. This comment was most definitely aimed at Max
~~~~~

Snowy weaved through Max's legs as though to agree.

Aurora told Max she would see him again soon. Once she reached home, she leaned on her windowsill and looked out at the city, and heard a crow caw in the background.

And then Snowy spit out the red herring toy in front of Aurora's lap.

"I'm sure we'll find the first clue to our next mystery soon," Aurora said with a smile.

The Blackout and the Poly-Gones

The lights went out

We heard a shout

People were scared

Nothing to be spared

Aurora knows who

Prologue

"This soundtrack is ghastly. Appalling. Outrageous… " Aurora flipped through a worn-out thesaurus as she looked for a properly fitting word to describe the show she was watching on her television.

Snowy sat on her lap and meowed her agreement.

"Even I could put this composer out of a job," Aurora told her cat. "All I need to do is write C-major chords, held for three hours straight. I wonder how the director ever agreed to this..." She continued to ramble about how in-proficient the production was while the climax of the movie ran on. And on and on and on.

"Just *cut* the *apple*," Aurora yelled at the cartoon characters on the TV. The seven short ones were presently off collecting pie crusts so the woman in the blue-yellow dress could cook a mediocre apple pie and gift it to her cruel stepmother. It was a commonly known movie that lots of people watched.

Someone stomped on the floor above, probably telling her to quiet down.

Aurora leaned over the side of her couch to find the remote in an effort to switch the channel, but before she could, an announcement popped up on the screen, flashing blue and green and a particular shade of white. Two news anchors took their seats in front of it and started to speak about *why* they'd chosen to disturb everyone's otherwise pleasant evening. *Well, more or less that,* Aurora thought to herself.

"*Public Service Announcement: Today is, as many of you know, a day in November. That has been so for 11 days, including today. In a minute more, the Verwood town clock will strike 11:11 PM: this marks the 11th anniversary of the polishing of the old copper on the new bell of the ...*"

"What a rambler," said Aurora to no one in particular.

They began a countdown within 30 seconds, towards 11:11:11 PM. Deciding to join in the once-a-year occasion, Aurora chanted the last eleven numbers.

"Eleven! Ten! Nine! Eight! No, Snowy, come back to my lap, it's … Five! Four! Three! *Snowy, don't eat that ice cream-* "

The lights went out as the TV personnel started to celebrate at "Zero!".

"Not again," Aurora muttered, stumbling over to the light switch in an effort to flip it back on. Recently, Snowy had gained a habit of jumping on the apartment's main power switch whenever Aurora was doing anything even remotely important.

But to her (Aurora's) astonishment, the lights didn't turn back on. As she turned around to face her window, she saw the rest of Verwood going down, block by block. Except for the crescent moon above them, the city was now under complete darkness.

The Plotting

As Master Quadratic surveyed the gathering crowd of one in front of himself, he mentally prepared his speech. He stood in front of the power supply box at V.E. (which stood for Verwood Electrical; not to be confused with Vermillion Elephants, which is a circus show across the world. It gets confused with Verwood Electrical over 79% of the time, and 5% of that ends in the creation of a Vermillion Donkey). It was not an ideal location for a speech, but he had to make do with the circumstances: a team of two, a city under darkness, and an imperative task at hand.

"As the girl detective has taken away our own precious Seg (with a peg leg), we must take from them something equally dear," said Quad. "As we have been spying on the crew in question, we already know what we must take, and what we must leave. You have the list, right?"

Perpen Dicular looked up, having the look on his face match one of a person giving a speech about penguin healthcare in the wrong language to the wrong group of people. "Sorry, what was that? I was trying to... err... umm... the box is on my *left* and- "

Quad shook his head in disappointment. "You have the list, *correct?* This will be the vertex of all our efforts. No plot would ever measure up to this. Tonight will be unparalleled!"

"Hopefully not," said Perp, "because I'm in it."

"Not what?"

"It will *not* be paralleled."

"I don't comprehend."

"It won't be paralleled because I'm Perpen- " Perp shook his head. "You know what, forget it." He shut the metal door of an electrical box. "Let us start, Master Quadratic," he suggested.

Quad smiled. "Let the city drown without light, as we steal everyone's lifeboats during the storm. And maybe we can get a right-angled cone, infinitely full of ice cream, afterwards."

Chapter 1

A flashlight in one hand, and the TV remote in the other, Aurora checked all the rooms in her apartment, calling for Snowy. "Where did you go, Snowy! Come back! This is not the time for running away!" Reaching a torrent of tears, which equaled that of the Niagara Falls, she slumped down on her couch. *Hopefully Snowy will come back from her little adventure soon...*

Aurora startled when she heard footsteps in the hallway outside her room. Deciding that, without Snowy, there wasn't a purpose to anything, she slowly approached the door. She picked up what she could only assume was a collapsible chair on her way there. Her fingers traced the width of the door before she found the deadbolt and pushed it out of lock. She spent a minute more locating the handle, and fingering it, wondering what horrors may await her outside...

Once again, she startled when the lights came on. Through the window, she could see, block by block, Verwood was once again illuminated. They were littering light into the sky once more, disturbing the flight paths of many ill-fated birds.

Aurora smiled at that. Perhaps Snowy would find one to eat...

Her hand slipped on the handle of the door when she leaned against it, and the door opened outwards. She fell right into two arms, which she later identified as connected to Max.

"Oh, umm, hi," Aurora stuttered. "Thanks for cat-ing... I mean, *catch*ing me." Once again, she wished she could have been Snowy: words deemed unnecessary, and she couldn't sound so dumb.

"No problem," Max said with a smile, setting her upright.

Aurora blushed from head to toe. When she caught herself grinning, she decided to say something. She realized she didn't know what to say. Thankfully, Max saved her from this awkward moment.

"I was walking around the block when the blackout happened, and wondered whether you were doing alright. You seem so." Max ran his fingers through his hair.

Aurora wondered how soft it would be. *What's wrong with me?* she chided herself after pushing the thought out of her head. "Umm, yeah. I'm alright."

"Snowy wasn't scared of the dark?" Max inquired.

Oh right. Snowy. Aurora felt like a fool. How could she have forgotten about *Snowy?* "I actually don't know where she is. I was looking for her when… " she trailed off as her mind went back to worrying about Snowy, who might wander away to the next random person who ran clinical trials in the park at midnight. Aurora cracked her knuckles in worry.

"Snowy is probably fine," Max reassured Aurora.

Aurora nodded nervously. "I hope so." She glanced behind herself. "Would you like to come in?"

They both searched Aurora's apartment for Snowy, and every so often, Max would comment on one of the knick-knacks that Aurora had collected over the years: A pen from Arial Times, an SD card to a Squirrel Assassins game, and the Egyptian necklace replica. Max even said that Aurora's scarlet-bead bracelet was quaint and elegant.

Most of Aurora's side of the conversation consisted of blushing and stuttering.

They had first covered the sitting room, then Max checked the kitchen while Aurora went off to her bedroom. She found the window wide open, the wind billowing the pale, lavender curtains around it like a ghost. Aurora frowned as she closed it before moving towards her bed. There was a lump under her blanket, and she approached it with caution. She poked it with a plastic hanger.

It didn't move.

She poked it again, and heard a creaking noise. Looking to her left, she saw that it was only Max, opening the door slowly, and still no sign of Snowy. Aurora turned back to the lump, and pulled off the blanket, revealing... her pillow.

Aurora shook her head in dismay as she folded her blanket carefully, then moved the pillow back into place. However, when she did the latter task, she noticed a slip of paper. It had been hidden under the pillow case.

The note said:

Solve for X
We wish you neither good luck, nor fun,
in search of your Snowy.
-The Poly-Gones

Flashes of a woman holding them hostage on the turret of Detective Aeyto's house flew through her mind; memories of a labyrinth and maniacal mathematicians, too.

Chapter 2

~~Caroit~~

He was the picture of serenity: wearing one-piece pajamas and a placid expression on his face. The lights were off and the ceiling fan made a near-silent whirring sound as it spun. Until it stopped.

Caroit was sensitive to everything, or so he claimed. A good case study of this is whenever his ceiling fan stops spinning: He throws off his blanket immediately and rounds his legs over the edge of the bed before starting to grumble about the lack of fresh air flow.

In this particular instance, the fan was out because of a city-wide blackout, so Caroit had to rummage through his bedside table for a flashlight. Realizing he didn't have anything but carrot-shaped stress toys, he trudged down the stairs and to the kitchen. He cast annoyed glares towards where Chief Tweety of Law and Order Green 2.0 was squawking off its head, and had half a mind to throw something at it. Perhaps a flashlight would shut it up. If only Caroit had a flashlight at that moment.

He was in the process of finding batteries (because the single flashlight he had found was devoid of them) when he heard a 7th-grader's voice behind him say, "Uncle Caroit, I found one already."

Caroit turned around to see a bright light, and behind it, his nephew Bean Green. It was something expected, since his sister Cel and her son were staying for a few weeks, but under the circumstances Caroit jumped up onto the table and let out a squeal.

(On a side note, when Green Bean showed a recording of this event to Aurora later, she was entertained by it until Caroit confiscated the only known copies of it.)

Once he'd gained composure, Caroit grabbed the flashlight from Green Bean's hand and used it to lead the way to his bedroom. Green Bean was chattering along about the bird-feed full of squiggly worms, how fascinating it was, and how he would bet on a friend eating it.

Chief Tweety 2.0 had somehow escaped from her cage, no doubt with help from Green Bean, and was now flying around the house and sitting on things. It's been thought odd how mildly this irritated Caroit. However, when Chief Tweety 2.0 sat on a tall leafy houseplant; the stalk slowly bent under the yellow bird's weight until the bird itself was supported by Caroit's head, which was directly below the plant and directly above the rest of his body.

He had to barely sigh, a wan expression across his face: the flustered, negative aura sent Chief Tweety flying across the hall to one of the secluded rooms downstairs.

Caroit peeked into Cel's room; she seemed to be passed out across her bed, but when Green Bean yelled at his mother, she sat up straight before giving Green Bean a sharp glare and telling Caroit to take care of "it," whatever "it" was.

Back in his bedroom, Caroit ran the dim stream of light over the walls, still squinting to see anything in the feeble light, when the electricity came back on. The ceiling fan started to whir once more, and Green Bean flipped a switch so the room illuminated in a whitish-light.

Caroit, meanwhile, stood in the middle of his room with a blank expression on his face, which slowly started to grow into extreme annoyance and sadness. It was a unique mix, certainly.

"Good night, Uncle Caroit," Green Bean said, bouncing on the bed and twanging Caroit's mustache before running out the bedroom door.

But all Caroit could process was that his old revolvers, usually mounted on the wall, were now gone. When he turned to wish his nephew a good night, he only saw a slip of paper floating to the ground. It said:

> *Solve for X*
> *No more shooting at things until then,*
> *Green Carrot Detective.*
> *-The Poly-Gones*

Caroit frowned as ripped off his pajamas in one quick stroke, revealing his police uniform, complete with his new Sudwig 192s in their respective holsters.

Chapter 3

Fazed by the whirl of events she'd been through, Aurora paced around the kitchen, now lit up by the returned electricity, pitching possibilities of where the Poly-Gones might have taken Snowy. Max, knowing the little bit he did about the Poly-Gones, gave his point of view on each proposition.

The ring of the phone, which was set on the side of the otherwise empty dining table, startled both of them. Aurora was the first to it, and she clearly recognized Katrina's voice on the other end of it.

"*He's.. gone!*" she was saying in a frantic rush.

"Who, Shaggy-Dog?" Aurora asked.

It sounded like Katrina was closing and locking all the windows in her house. "*No, it's Jerry! And there's a note from the Poly-Gones.*"

"Does it say 'Solve for X?'" Max offered. Aurora hadn't noticed that he'd been standing so close-by and felt her heart beating louder than ever before. She only hoped Max couldn't hear it.

"*Yes, it does.*" Then Katrina inquired whose tenor voice she'd heard.

Aurora proffered the phone to Max to explain because her cellphone had also started to ring at that moment. Answering it, she heard Caroit's incessant grumbling, and in the midst of it, something about his revolvers, the Poly-Gones, and the three hostile words which summed up most of the night: "Solve for X."

Another call came to Aurora's home phone, so she set down her conversation and moved behind Max. She urged him to pick up the new call.

"Goodbye, Katrina, and I hope to meet you and Shaggy-Dog soon!" he said before greeting the next person with a: "Hi, this is Aurora's residence. How may I help you?"

"Is this the wrong number? Or did you just get a gruff maid?"

Max turned to Aurora, the phone angled downwards. "Do you know anyone with this voice? Sounds like a prank call."

Aurora sighed. "It sounds like Aleks." She took the phone into her own hands, and asked what the matter was, ignoring Max's unbated scrutiny of "This new and suspicious character, Aleks."

"Some no-brained fellow has committed a crime of vandalism over here," Aleks said across the phone. *"I had half the mind to push him down an elevator shaft, but there were no elevators around."*

"This isn't really the time for jokes. I need to go now, Snowy's missing - "

"It's really big graffiti too: all over the wall. White spray paint on some ancient brick-work on Tom's house. It's so terrible that Tom's duck got all riled up and went missing."

"Aleks, I need to go to - "

"And what's more, it's a big 'X'..No meaning at all, just a random shape meant to mess up the fragile environment of Tom's duck's pond-vicinity. Or something like that, I wasn't paying attention."

"I - wait, an 'X'?"

"Why? Does it mean anything to you? Or perhaps to your man-maid?"

"That's not… it was Max."

"Who's Max?"

"That doesn't matter right now."

"What if he's the one who vandalized - "

"We're coming over right now, Aleks," Aurora said. "Don't go anywhere." And she kept down the phone, and moved to a regular routine: grab her coat, keys, car…

62

Chapter 4

The whole group, Katrina, Shaggy-Dog, Caroit, Aurora, and Max, plus Tom, Aleks, and Natalia, stood near the large outerwall of Tom's mansion with the large, white X on it. Between them, they'd lost a cat, a duck, a husband, and a particularly wonderful set of revolvers, all to the Poly-Gones.

There wasn't much to do: a marking on the wall didn't actually help them, nor did it give any real clues. After the first minute of hectic worrying, they'd all taken to pleasant chatter regarding what they'd done over the weekend, etc.

It wasn't hard for Aurora to notice that Max and Aleks purposefully stayed on opposite sides of the group. Natalia, on the other hand, was fraternizing with "the enemy," or at least that was what Aleks was telling Aurora in that moment.

"Is this your way of bringing me some competition, Aurora?" Aleks asked with a cocky smile.

Obviously oblivious to the nuanced inflections of Aleks' voice, Aurora asked, "What competition? You can *both* be my friends."

Aleks opened his mouth to say something, then promptly closed it as Caroit (followed by a wet Shaggy-Dog) walked up to them.

"*Vat* are we all doing here?" Caroit asked them, dark circles forming under his eyes. It seemed like he had something small and orange in his hand, and he squeezed it with vigor.

"The X," Aurora said, *must* mean something! I mean, it's so big and - " Everyone had now turned to listen to Aurora's half-baked speech. She took a deep breath to compose herself, and saw Max give her a thumbs-up from somewhere in the crowd. "The Poly-Gones have told us to solve for X, and conveniently, have given us the X: big, bold, and white against the brick facade. We know the Poly-Gones, no matter how cruel they seem, are true to their words. They like puzzles, and like watching us try to solve them.

"There is nothing more to this: all of us waiting in Tom's backyard in the cold, dark, middle of the night is because we *know* that the Poly-Gones want us to be here. We have no choice but to play along." Aurora considered the sad looks on everyone's faces and decided they all needed to do *something* while waiting. "Let's be on the lookout for them. They must come from one of the sides. Surely not from underground like a Pika," she glanced at the dirt around her feet, "and not from above like a bird."

To emphasize this last point, she looked up, and as everyone followed her gaze to see…

"That's an X," Katrina pointed out.

Surely, it was an X: hundreds of stars had been densely put into a formation so, from their angle, it looked like an X, bright and clear against the midnight sky.

"Flaming spheres of hydrogen," Aurora muttered as she craned her neck to better see the sparkling new stars. "How on earth did they install new…"

They started to move, collectively, towards the east.

"They're drones!" Max exclaimed with as much excitement as an eager puppy. "I've read all about them! Flying robots - wow this is cool!"

The whole group followed the moving drones, keeping their eyes on the shimmering light cast down from them, and made their way into a heavily wooded environment. Twice, Shaggy-Dog walked into a tree, but he shook it off eagerly and then bounded along.

"I know this is terrible to think about," Katrina said near Aurora, "but it's a beautiful sight. I only wish Jerry was here to see it, too."

Even though Aurora agreed about it being abhorrent, she too admired the precision with which the X-constellation was drawn in the sky, just for them.

Chapter 5

Their drone-gazing parade ended in a small clearing within the forest. Aurora didn't notice this until she bumped into Caroit. It wasn't a result of her not paying attention, but rather the result of Shaggy-Dog bumping into her with all his mass. It was also due to an unexpected bump on the leaf-covered forest floor.

At present, the bump made a little noise. "Mmmm hmm MMMM."

Aurora took a step back.

"Mmmhmm mhmmm mmmm." That was Caroit making an attempt to speak in whatever language the bump was speaking in. He pointed his multitude of guns at the bump, and then demanded, "Put your hands up!"

"MMMMMMMMM HMMMMMMM."

"I think the bump wants something," Max suggested, kneeling by it, and moving to pull out the gag and push away the decaying leaves from the bump's face.

Before he could, however, someone called from the other end of the clearing. Their face was not as visible as it would have been under the light of the drones (which were now all off), and thus most definitely not recognizable. "Perp, what in the name of complex mathematics are you doing *there?*" He called.

"MMMMMMMMMMM."

"Could you please stop keeping him hostage?" The man from the other end of the clearing called again.

"Who are you?" asked Aurora.

"And *vat* are you doing here?" Caroit added.

Behind them, Aleks sounded like he was trying hard to repress a giggle. At the end, he failed to accomplish it and burst into a fit of laughter. Speculation leads to the laughter being induced either by a rare bug's sting, which could make anyone laugh to asphyxiation, or, given the current circumstances, it was more likely that his laughter is due to Caroit's strategic deployment of his classic phrase.

"MM HMMMMMMMMMMMMMMMMMM." It sounded like the bump - *Perp* - was arguing about something. He must have realized that there was no reason why the gag was in his mouth, except that he didn't know where else to put it, so he pulled it out.

From the other end of the clearing, the man said something quietly to the space behind him, which was very obviously occupied by nothing other than trees and a few deranged birds, who were squawking their beaks off. He yelled over the cacophony, "Hand over Perp or you will fail in solving for X!"

"You're with the Poly-Gones?" Max asked, taking a cautious step closer to the man.

The latter chuckled. "Not with them: I lead them. I am Master Quadratic." His tone grew grave. "Your friends are long gone, and some of my other…" He paused. "Why am I even telling you this?"

"Because you're a stereotypical villain who lays out their plans so the heroes can *intercept* it?" Aurora offered.

Although unheard to anyone else, Caroit murmured, "We *are* heroes…"

Meanwhile, Master Quadratic's gaze turned to Perp. "Get up and come over here, Perp."

Perp sat up and wiped the dirt off his eyes.

"He's not going anywhere," Max interceded, stepping on the tail of Perp's shirt.

Master Quadratic took out a pad of paper and wrote something on it with a pen, then tossed both to the empty space behind him. "Your friends are long gone unless you agree to concur and act in accordance with… umm…"

"To consent to let me go," Perp finished.

Aurora looked over all her friends, each missing someone dear to their heart. She glanced at Perp, who was muttering something about spies being overrated. "Let him go, M-," she started, but by then, someone cried out from behind the bushes across the clearing.

"Those are not regular bushes! I should have suspected the mobile-bushes," Caroit said proudly to everyone. "I told them that they should not be released to the public... "

"It was a bad idea to give your hostages pens," Jerry's voice yelled. Everyone swiveled on their heels to see a pen tossed from the bush and hit Quad squarely on the forehead.

Quad gave a small squeal before marching across the clearing to Perp. "Why did you leave them in the forest, imbecile! I told you to hide them somewhere."

"You see, Master, I thought that this was somewhere," Perp said shakily, "but- "

"Technically, he is right," Aurora intervened, "because everywhere is somewhere including nowhere, which is- "

Shaggy-Dog must have felt bored at that point, because he leaped across 3 meters, launching himself towards Aurora. She ducked, so Shaggy-Dog, with slobber dripping out of his mouth, landed on the head of Master Quadratic, who still seemed in awe.

"That launch angle for the parabolic trajectory was calculated perfectl- ACK! Perp, help me, I'm... "

The Arrest

~~Caroit~~

Covered in icky slobber, Perp and Quad huddled under the nearest tree, with three guns and Caroit's frown all pointing at them. Behind that was over half of Verwood's police force, plus some of the federal police, but none of that equaled the rage boiling within Caroit.

"You broke my window's lock!"

"Well, yes, but- " shivered Master Quadratic.

"You entered my house!"

"I just- " quivered Master Quadratic.

"You took my guns!"

"And I found this," Perp said, tossing Caroit a small, orange, carrot-shaped stress toy.

Caroit glanced behind him, then slipped his guns into their respective holsters. "I will be back. I will have my revenge. I will- "

He was cut short of his vengeance-speech by Chief Don Utt, who placed a fat hand on Caroit's shoulder. "Okay, there, Detective Green. You're done for now, eh? Go and be reunited with… with your… guns?"

Caroit sighed and stumbled off, towards where everyone else was busy reuniting. The ropes had been cut from Jerry's wrists, and he was embracing Katrina warmly. Aleks and Natalia were discussing something off to the side. Detective Aeyto was hugging his duck close to his chest.

"Apparently, the duck had swallowed a federal tracking device, and activated it when they were kidnapped. Smart quacker, hmm?" Max told Caroit, catching his stares. "Teaches criminals to drug the pets too, next time, and not just the humans."

Caroit had responded with a nod, then trudged onward. He couldn't find Aurora, Max, or Snowy anywhere, nor his own revolvers. He had trekked a good length when he was caught unawares by a 7th grader, who had all of Caroit's kidnapped revolvers in a loose holster. He'd leaped out of the bushes as Caroit turned a corner, causing the latter to trip over a gnarly root.

"Uncle Caroit!" There was a lot of enthusiasm in the young boy's voice as he tackle-hugged his uncle dearly.

"Bean." Meanwhile, Caroit had lost most of his enthusiasm due to the gnarly root which was poking him in his back. But when he really took in the bright, excited smile of Green Bean with his small arms wrapped around Caroit's neck, and Cel standing away in the distance and grinning at them both, Caroit decided to hug his nephew back.

He was glad to have them.

~~Aurora~~

Aurora was not far from the others, albeit hidden from their view. In her hands, she gingerly held Snowy, and Max stood next to her, petting the fluffy, white cat. It was quiet but for the murmurs of others in their immediate surroundings.

Snowy meowed, causing Aurora to sigh in relief. "I'm so glad she's safe," Aurora muttered.

She barely noticed when Max wrapped an arm around her and pulled her in close. Naturally, she tilted her head, rested it on his shoulder, and looked out, into the dark forest. And she only *just* noticed when Max kissed her on the cheek.

Head whipping to a side and stepping back clumsily, she almost dropped Snowy. "I - "

"Sorry if - "

"No, I mean - "

Max blinked, breaking the nervous eye contact they'd been keeping. "Did I read you wrong?"

All this time, Aurora had been thinking Max *didn't* like her, and wished only that he reciprocate her feelings. "No…" But she was startled, surely.

"I meant that… Aurora, I didn't... " The expression on his face waned as he panicked.

Before Aurora could speak again, Detective Tom Aeyto approached the scene and began to loquaciously praise Max's detective work.

"Max, I think I'm going to go inside to check on the others," Aurora said quickly. She slowly swiveled on her heels and walked back to Tom's mansion. Her pace gradually picked up until she was breathing heavily and near the entrance.

She remembered the path to the kitchen and decided to go there. *What was wrong, she liked Max! Why did she have to freak out so much and... and...* Aurora wondered whether she ought to go back outside, but the air carried the scents of hot chocolate, and she decided she should process the event before going to Max once again.

~~Aleks~~

Through the glass-paned door of the kitchen, Aleks spotted Aurora walking in. Her pants were splattered with wet mud and her expression looked a mix of grumpy and tired. Snowy trailed behind her. Aleks decided to take to Aurora a mug of hot chocolate; a purple one specially chosen for her favorite color.

"Why are you soggy?" he asked, protectively draping a towel over Aurora's shivering shoulders and guiding her towards the dim candle-lit dining room. In the center stood an antique dining table which currently housed stacks of his mother's fancy china and a fine layer of dust.

"Hmm?" Aurora asked over the mug, pulling the towel closer. It was nice and warm. She looked down at herself, and seemed to realize her dirt-covered appearance. "It was muddy and drizzling a bit. I ran over here."

"What, away from your new man-maid?" Aleks sat down in the chair beside her, using the edge of her towel to dab away at the excess water on her forehead.

Aurora frowned and set down the mug, wiping off the milk-mustache with the back of her hand. "It isn't funny." Yet she could not suppress her smile.

"Well..." Aleks looked around himself and fumbled with an arbitrary button ambisinistrously. "Just know I'm here if you need anything."

"I know Aleks."Aurora wanly smiled. Aleks was too good to her. "You always seem to know how to make me smile. You're a wonderful… a wonderful person." He was most definitely annoying at times but she didn't mind it. In fact, she kind of liked it when he was joking around. It was an exciting day when she met him, dull without. Aurora could not understand why he wouldn't say something, and instead tried to maintain eye contact. His eyes were a nice color. Her smile popped up again.

Why won't she just say something? Aleks thought to himself. *When will she think of me as... as something more?* He tried to look anywhere but directly at her and ended up spotting Max peering through one of the doorways, frowning at the hand Aleks had placed on Aurora's shoulder.

Max seemed to mutter something before moving onward.

Aurora showed no notice of Max's quick visit, so Aleks assumed she hadn't noticed.

Max seemed to have known something Aleks didn't. Aleks wished he knew, then decided that he was happier to be sitting besides Aurora in the moment.

"That was good hot chocolate," Aurora said, breaking the line of thought Aleks had. She patted Aleks' hand, which still rested on Aurora's shoulder, as a means to gain his attention.

"Hmm?" Aleks asked. "Oh, the hot chocolate. Natalia made it."

At that moment, another door opened up and Natalia ran in. "The police are all leaving, and the clouds have parted. We can see the stars more clearly. You should come out now!" She then registered that Aleks and Aurora must have been talking about something important, so she made some noise like "yippee" and ran out.

Aleks blushed insanely and wished Aurora didn't notice. Or no, he *did* wish she noticed. But he didn't want to come off as needy. Or to push her into anything. No, he wanted to -

"Let's go out!" Aurora grabbed Aleks' hand and pulled him along. They soon made it to the wrap-around porch in the front of the house. Police cars wailed in the distance, their little lights making a sort of weaving snake on the winding roads that led out of the forest and back to the city.

The night fell silent, leaving nothing but natural stars twinkling in the sky. Aurora pulled her towel tighter around her shoulders.

Aleks wondered if someone living further north could have seen the Aurora Borealis in this lighting. He wondered whether the northern lights would ever be more captivating than the girl standing next to him.

Aurora intertwined their fingers at the present, and it was all Aleks could do to not say something stupid.

Beside him, Tomato patted his precious, round duck on its head three times, then waved to nothing in particular.

"Bye bye, Poly-Gones!"

Appendix
Cast Trivia

Learn more about the residents of Verwood.
Alphabetized by first name.

Aleks Kovsky

My Unconventional Hobbies

Taking strolls at 4AM

Taking strolls at midnight

Avoiding elevators at all costs

Helping damsels in distress who are hanging onto broken elevators with their last shred of strength

Coincidentally running into a detective named Aurora Frost

Avoiding cats named Snowy

~~Bean Green~~ Green Bean

Green Bean's Tips on Life

If you ever find yourself to be the sole nephew of Detective Caroit Green, and if you're talking to him:

1. Don't call him Carrot (unless you're Auntie Aurora Frost or Snowy the Cat)
2. If you see the words "*Green Carrot Detective wuz here*" written on the wall, it means that one of my uncle's numerous fans has visited that place.
3. Always compliment his mustache - unless you're me, in which case you must twang it and watch it oscillate.

If you're in math class, and you say "crocodile" enough times, you're bound to get at least one question right. For example, if the math teacher asks: "According to this chart, which amphibian has the least population in this lake?"

If you say crocodile, the teacher will either tell you: "nice try" or say "you see, students, Green Bean is such an amazingly diligent worker. You should all be more like him."

According to my statistics, the crocodile scheme works about 30 meters - I mean, 30 percent - better than actually trying to solve the problem.

If your mother's name is Celery, and everyone calls her "Cel", make sure you remind the cashier at *No-No Pomo* that your mom isn't "sell"ing anything. It's just her name.

Pigeon poop falling on your head is not a very good experience. I'd give it 0.42 out of 5 stars.

"Cool Bean" = signing off

Amarinda Helvetica

The Verwood Collection
brought to you by Amarinda Helvetica, ft. Fools

1 Grand Piano (returned)
? Various Jewels
1 Ring from The Helvetica Household
1 Diamond Bracelet from the Helvetica Jewelry Store
1 Pole-vaulting stick
1 Sapphire from the Verwood Museum
372 hours of tax-payer money, gone to police detective work
1 Lancelot Helvetica's heart

Aurora Frost

VPD File on Miss Aurora Frost

Name: Aurora Frost
Age: 19
Address: 316 Verwood Grove Apartments, Verwood
Current Occupation: Private Investigator and Part-Time Instigator
Physical Description: Black hair, Brown eyes
Height: Tall enough to eat cookies from the jar in the top cabinet (with provided step stool)
Companions: Preposterous feline, Pink playwright, Red haired psychologist, Egoistic mafia relative

Known Cases:
1. Helvetica Piano and Jewels
2. Parking Garage explosion
3. Pet Store with Bananana #1
4. Shaggy-Dog kidnapping
5. No-No Coco Auditions
6. Stolen Quokka from Smiles and Snuggles Zoo [overseas]
7. Attempted Murder at the Theatre
8. Kidnapping at Detective Aeyto's basement *(not closed)*
9. Verwood Museum - Egyptian Exhibit theft
10. Yodeling Cult at Beach
11. Attacks at Verwood Secondary School reunion
12. Helvetica Jewelry Store theft *(not closed)*
13. Missing person: Corporate scandal with Nuts and Bolts
14. Chair-attacks for inclusion of rare birds in Verwood Aviary
15. Viola Mafia
16. Missing persons: Rural area outside Verwood
17. Foreign Dignitary Poisoning
18. Local Party-theft
19. Verwood Museum - Blue Sapphire theft *(not closed)*
20. Missing Cats *(completed file not turned in)*
21. Bank Robbery
22. Various kidnappings

Detective Caroit Green

Also known as "The Green Carrot Detective."

Leetle Caroit Green and the Pencil Scheme

"Good morning," greeted the teacher.

Caroit Green did a fancy hat trick, his black bowlers' hat landing right atop his head after doing a flip in the air. "The morning does not seem so good to me," Caroit told his teacher, "but I guess *eet* is your opinion that *eet* is a good morning." Young Caroit had a thick accent from his parents, who'd lived somewhere in Eastern Europe.

He took a seat in the second row, right in front of his arch-enemy, Brock O. Li. He was just a really rude, snobby boy who didn't *understand* the simple things in life.

"Hello again, *Little Carrot*," Brock said, using Caroit's designated nickname.

Caroit smiled coyly. "Hi to you too, *Large Brock*." Caroit turned back to his books - *7th grade English* was on top of the pile, followed by some *Geometry* and *History of Detectives*. He set his pencils in a neat line, and used an eraser to block them from rolling off the desk.

"I need a pencil," he felt Brock's finger on his shoulder, poking him between his neck and his bony shoulder blade.

"Okay! Okay!" Caroit told Brock. He meant, of course he'd give Brock a pencil, but Brock never really specified *when* so… Caroit started flipping through his homework and making a stack on the left side of his desk, just in time for the teacher to collect it.

Then he heard their math teacher pause at Brock's desk, right behind him. "Do you have a pencil to write your name on these?" she asked.

Brock's anger radiated through the classroom and sent an undulating wave of fear through Caroit's skin as Brock gritted his teeth and said, "No."

Caroit braced himself for the next jab on his shoulder, but it never came.

"I need a pencil. Now," Brock said, leaning forward so much that his desk squished lanky little Caroit between his desk and his chair.

"Okay," Caroit said, slowly picking up the first pencil he saw. But then he swiveled in his chair to face Brock." How do I know you will give it back? I need insurance."

Brock snatched the pencil out of Caroit's hand and simply said, "I won't give it back. That's my guarantee."

Caroit frowned, then crossed his arms as he huffed, then scrawled his name across the next worksheet his teacher handed him. As he worked through the first sets of linear equations, a sort of plan formed in his mind. He glanced back at Brock, who seemed to be looking out the window, before he picked up another pencil.

Caroit made sure that the teacher was working at her desk, and not watching, before he flicked his own pencil directly upward. And when it fell, it hit Caroit on his head.

"Oh no!" one of the kids near Caroit said.

This had caused the teacher to look up, and her focus locked on Brock, who was still looking out the window, twirling Caroit's other pencil in his hand.

The teacher walked over to Brock, and Caroit decided that he should work on his poker face since he could barely contain his laughter.

"What's up?" Brock asked the teacher, unaware of the pencil Caroit had launched into the air mere moments ago.

The teacher muttered something before putting one hand on her hip. Her other hand pointed to the class's door. A sign that *someone* was going to be in big trouble.

As Brock sauntered by, Caroit knew who was going to take the blame for this little stunt. "The ceiling," Caroit said as Brock paused near his desk.

"What about it?" Brock asked.

"That's what's up," Caroit told him.

Caroit, as always, finished his work early, and rolled a coin over his fingers as he watched the clock, counting down the seconds until this class was over. The bell rang, and Caroit tucked his coin in his pocket.

He even winked at Brock on his way out.

Celery Green

Excerpts from Cel's voicemails to Caroit.
(Caroit replied to most of these voicemails.)

Caroit, have you fed your bird? How's Chief Tweety of Law and Order Green doing?

Caroit, why is Bean telling me that he rode a llama with your permission? Call me back.

Caroit, let me know if you need more stress toys. I saw a packet of seven of them for sale.

Caroit, here's a mystery for you. Why is Bean so persistent on growing a mustache? He said something about twanging mustaches being "hip" but I'm not sure what that means. Call me back once you solve it.

Harley Darley

Also known as "the rhyming boy."

Harley Darley's Daring Adventure to the VPD

Harley Darley boisterously visited the Verwood Police Department on a fine and sunny afternoon. He went straight to the Homicide and Grand Theft floor and upon locating Detective Caroit Green's desk, took a seat in front of it. On the ground, legs crossed. Before Harley got to meet Caroit, another old man walked by.

"Who are you, kid?" asked the old man. He seemed grumpy and not wholesome.

"I'm pretty mid."

"What does that mean?" the old man said, the sheen on his forehead growing more sheen-ey.

Harley Darley decided to point it out. "Your forehead's got sheen."

"Do you know who I am?"

"You're an old man."

The old man's eyes narrowed and he was at the last ounce of his patience, it seemed. "I'm Chief Don Utt."

"A definite nut."

Chief Utt kneeled on the floor to get level with Harley, who was now standing. "Kid, why don't you see yourself out."

"Don't make me pout." For effect, Harley pouted.

"You're pouting." Chief Utt pointed out, not knowing what else to say.

"You're shouting." Harley, on the other hand, was calm and composed. He saw Caroit walking in from the stairwell and ran over to the tall lanky detective.

"Yes, rhyming boy?" Caroit asked. He seemed in a good mood today.

"I'm not here to annoy."

"Well then, what is it?"

"I solved your case, Mr. Carrot." With that, Harley dropped a small piece of paper into Caroit's hand and took the stairs by two as he exited the Verwood Police Department. As Caroit would soon figure out, the small piece of paper was actually Harley Darley reporting on when he saw Chief Utt take *two* samples of strawberry ice cream from the local ice cream parlor.

A true crime.

Jerry Mousey Bumbly

As many of you know, I used to be a world-famous table-tennis player for a very long time. At least, it felt like a very long time. According to the calendar, it was a total of two days, during which I managed to win my house and four cans of pink paint. There was also a chemistry textbook involved, although I do not currently recall why.

The four cans of pink paint later led to me meeting Katrina Mousey Bumbly as she was the highest bidder when I was trying to auction off the paint at the annual Verwood Chemistry Festival. Of course, regarding Katrina and myself, our middle and last names were the same by coincidence.

We quickly adopted our son Shaggy-Dog Mousey Bumbly, who brought great joy to both of our lives in a furry little package.

Katrina Mousey Bumbly

Also known as "Kitty."

       I once attended the Verwood Chemistry Festival, and I remember there were four very pretty cans of pink paint being auctioned off by a handsome young man. It was Jerry! Of course, I did not know his name at the time. I remeumber I held up my bidding card of *Forty Seven Dollars and Fifty Two Cents* during the event and the joy of running up to the stage to claim my four cans of pink paint.

I wanted to paint a bookshelf with it, then paint all the books in the bookshelf pink as well. However, I got married to Jerry very soon after and instead we used the pink paint to paint our kitchen.

We quickly adopted our son Shaggy-Dog Mousey Bumbly, who brought great joy to both of our lives in a furry little package. Shaggy-Dog sat in one of the half-used cans of paint when he was a puppy and has ever after maintained the chic fashion statement of remaining in a shade of pink.

Lancelot Helvetica

From Lance's most recent letter to his mother.

Dear Mother,

I have found myself in the basement of... oh wait I'm at home. I'm in my house. I mean, your house. I hope you didn't notice. Just know that I love you and also I need $200 because Randi took all our money to join the circus again or something.

Your favorite son,
Lance

Max Roosters

Before I came to Verwood, I only saw the city through its newspaper. I remember the day I read the story of a young woman solving the piano theft at the Helvetica's mansion. It was special to me because I recalled that a young man a few farms over had a similar last name. I visited that house to inquire but the door was locked and the windows drawn. When I returned home, my parents told me to go tend to the chickens, as I did every evening (and morning and afternoon).

It was that moment. That was when I realized how much I'd prefer going to the city. I decided to become a psychologist and moved to Verwood. I studied psychology under Dr. Nerz Doktor, who is arguably the most educated person in Verwood. In my freetime, I worked shifts at Nuts and Bolts for a minimal wage, and occasionally ran into the same young detective woman I'd initially read about in the paper around town.

At least, that's the story I tell everyone.

Natalia Kovsky

I really don't like plates.

Dr. Nerz Doktor

"Arguably the most educated person in Verwood." *bakawk.*
Will edit genes for a small fee.

Shaggy-Dog Mousey Bumbly

"Woof." Picks up a pink cup of tea and takes a sip. Translated: "As the elegant, poised, and educated son of Jerry Mousey Bumbly and Katrina Mousey Bumbly, I have amended all legal documents pertaining to our house to eventually leave the property under my name. Thank you and please." Picks up a pink cup of tea and takes a sip.

Snowy Frost

Also known as "Preposterous Feline."

"Meow."
Translated: "Meow."

Detective Tom Aeyto

Poem by Tom,
made with love and a top-secret poem-auto-generator software
found on a secret server.

Big mansion on cement hill
Pretty scenery sky and benches
Roses blooming in worm
Sunshine in sunrise
Duck pond waves
Pole

~The End!~

Stay tuned for Aurora's next mysteries!

If you enjoyed this book, please take a few moments to write a review of it.

Thank you!

Books in this Series

Find the Mysteries of Frost Series on Amazon:
https://www.amazon.com/dp/B09WRPKHYR

About

Jana A. Bee - Author

Mysteries of Frost is Jana's first novel-series. She is a part-time novelist, and part-time instigator, but time doesn't part for her to keep up with the myriad other projects she works on. In her free time, she reads, writes, laughs, and plays instruments. She enjoys logical and mathematical puzzles and keeps a notebook of witty sentences and events from her life and experiences.

Instagram: @jana.a.bee
Email: jana.a.bee.mof@gmail.com

Jo N. Bee - Illustrator

Jo is a kind, caring, friendly, outgoing person. She likes to have long walks on the beach while listening to various genres of music and just generally thinking about anything. In her free time, she likes to draw and make artistic comments about other artists. She also likes to bake, her favorites being cherry pies or lemon cake with blueberries.

www.ingramcontent.com/pod-product-compliance
Lightning Source LLC
Chambersburg PA
CBHW020125180726
47992CB00020B/2510